The Fish Is Me

bathtime rhymes

Selected by Neil Philip
Illustrated by Claire Henley

CLARION BOOKS

New York

For Philippa, Julia, and Nathan
water babies all three

Bathtime

I love a bath,
I love a bath—
It is such jolly fun.
There's nothing like
A bath for laughs,
I'm always having one.
I like to splash,
I like to splosh
In water nice and hot.
I like to wash
And wash and wash—
I love it such a lot.
And when it's over
And I'm clean
It's really such a shame,
So out I go
And play with mud—
So I can bathe again!

Mark Burgess

Soap

Just look at those hands!
Did you actually think
That the dirt would come off, my daughter,
By wiggling your fingers
Around in the sink
And slapping the top of the water?

Just look at your face!
Did you really suppose
Those smudges would all disappear
With a dab at your chin
And the tip of your nose
And a rub on the back of one ear?

You tell me your face
And your fingers are *clean?*
Do you think your old Dad is a dope?
Let's try it again
With a different routine.
This time we'll make use of the soap!

Martin Gardner

Trouble Bubble Bath

There's trouble in my bubble bath—
It's time to disembark.
Beneath the soap and suds there swims
The cleanest, meanest shark.

Douglas Florian

Naughty Soap Song

Just when I'm ready to
Start on my ears,
That is the time that my
Soap disappears.

It jumps from my fingers and
Slithers and slides
Down to the edge of the
Tub, where it hides.

And acts in a most diso-
Bedient way
AND THAT'S WHY MY SOAP'S
GROWING
THINNER EACH DAY.

Dorothy Aldis

Water Everywhere

There's water on the ceiling,
And water on the wall,
There's water in the bedroom,
And water in the hall,
There's water on the landing,
And water on the stair,
Whenever Daddy takes a bath
There's water everywhere.

Valerie Bloom

Oh, No!

What's that sound?
Glug—glug—glug.
Barbie's hair's gone down the plug.

Neil Philip

Why Is It ?

Why is it
That,
In our bathroom,
It's not the dirtiest
Or the strongest
Who stay longest?
BUT
It always seems to be
The one who gets there
Just ahead
Of me.

Why is it
That people fret
When they're wet,
With loud cries
And soap in their eyes
And agonized howls,
Because they forget
Their towels?

Why is it that—
When *I'm* in the bath,
Steaming and dreaming,
My toes just showing
And the hot water flowing,
That other people
Yell and say,
"Are you there to stay
Or just on a visit?"

Why is it?

Max Fatchen

If I Were a Fish

Splash, splosh!
Whenever I wash
I wish and wish and wish
That I lived in the water all day long
Like a slithery, slippery fish.

Splash, splish!
If I were a fish
I wouldn't have to wash.
I wouldn't need soap or a towel or a sponge,
But I'd splish—
    And I'd splash—
        And I'd splosh!

Alison Winn

Slippery

The six-month child
Fresh from the tub
Wriggles in our hands.
This is our fish child.
Give her a nickname: Slippery.

Carl Sandburg

Washing

What is all this washing about,
Every day, week in, week out?
From getting up till going to bed,
I'm tired of hearing the same thing said.
Whether I'm dirty or whether I'm not,
Whether the water is cold or hot,
Whether I like it or whether I don't,
Whether I will or whether I won't,
"Have you washed your hands, and washed your face?"
I seem to *live* in the washing place.

Whenever I go for a walk or ride,
As soon as I put my nose inside
The door again, there's someone there
With a sponge and soap, and a lot they care
If I have something better to do,
"Now wash your face and your fingers too."

Before a meal is ever begun,
And after ever a meal is done,
It's time to turn on the waterspout.

Please, what *is* all this washing about?

John Drinkwater

Wash, Hands, Wash

Wash, hands, wash,
  Daddy's gone to plow.
If you want your hands washed,
  Have them washed now.

Traditional

Bath

Wash wash in the bath
even though I'm not dirty.
If I keep on washing every day
I'll be clean by the time I'm thirty.

Pauline Stewart

Bath Night

Some like bath night
    I
    DO
    NOT
     !

For the cold's so cold
And the hot's so hot,
And the soap goes slippering
Up my nose,
Into my eyes and
Between my toes;
The sponge goes splurge
And the floor gets wet,
And there's suds on the wall
And Nan's upset,
And the steam curls up
And the air looks white,
And it's not like day,
And it's not like night;
And then Nan says
I've had enough,
And the chair feels hard
And the towel feels rough,
And there's one thing that's funny
And I'll whisper what—
    Some
    Like
    Bath
    Night
But I . . . . ! ! ! !

Caryl Brahms

The Tub

My tub is an aquarium
In which the fish is me;
I like to think that I am some
Strange monster of the sea.

Sometimes a mighty whale I am,
The monarch of the deep,
And other times I am a clam
And almost fall asleep.

Then I become a sinking ship
That signals her distress
And tells of a disastrous trip
By yelling "SOS!"

And then I am a lifeboat, manned
By gallant lads and true,
I save myself from drowning and
I get a medal, too!

And then I hear my mother's shout,
That calls me back to shore,
And GEE! I have to clamber out
And be a boy once more!

George S. Chappell

Dirt Has Its Uses, Too

I don't ever wash,
whatever the weather—
it's only the dirt
that holds me together!

Neil Philip

Miss Susie Had a Baby

Miss Susie had a baby,
His name was Tiny Tim,
She put him in the bathtub
To see if he could swim.
He drank up all the water,
He ate up all the soap,
He tried to eat the bathtub
But it wouldn't go down his throat.

Miss Susie called the doctor,
The doctor called the nurse,
The nurse called the lady
With the alligator purse.
Out ran the doctor,
Out ran the nurse,
Out ran the lady
With the alligator purse.
And now Tiny Tim is home sick in bed
With soap in his throat and bubbles in his head.

Traditional

After a Bath

After my bath
I try, try, try
to wipe myself
till I'm dry, dry, dry.

Hands to wipe
and fingers and toes
and two wet legs
and a shiny nose.

Just think how much
less time I'd take
if I were a dog
and could shake, shake, shake.

Aileen Fisher

Granny Granny
Please Comb My Hair

Granny Granny
please comb my hair
you always take your time
you always take such care

You put me to sit on a cushion
between your knees
you rub a little coconut oil
parting gentle as a breeze

Mummy Mummy
she's always in a hurry-hurry
rush
she pulls my hair
sometimes she tugs

But Granny
you have all the time in the world
and when you're finished
you always turn my head and say
"Now who's a nice girl."

Grace Nichols